The Boxcar Children Mysteries

THE BOXCAR CHILDREN
SURPRISE ISLAND
THE YELLOW HOUSE MYSTERY
MYSTERY RANCH
MIKE'S MYSTERY
BLUE BAY MYSTERY
THE WOODSHED MYSTERY
THE LIGHTHOUSE MYSTERY
MOUNTAIN TOP MYSTERY
SCHOOLHOUSE MYSTERY
CABOOSE MYSTERY
HOUSEBOAT MYSTERY
SNOWBOUND MYSTERY
TREE HOUSE MYSTERY
BICYCLE MYSTERY
MYSTERY IN THE SAND
MYSTERY BEHIND THE WALL
BUS STATION MYSTERY
BENNY UNCOVERS A MYSTERY
THE HAUNTED CABIN MYSTERY
THE DESERTED LIBRARY MYSTERY
THE ANIMAL SHELTER MYSTERY
THE OLD MOTEL MYSTERY
THE MYSTERY OF THE HIDDEN PAINTING
THE AMUSEMENT PARK MYSTERY
THE MYSTERY OF THE MIXED-UP ZOO
THE CAMP-OUT MYSTERY
THE MYSTERY GIRL
THE MYSTERY CRUISE
THE DISAPPEARING FRIEND MYSTERY
THE MYSTERY OF THE SINGING GHOST
MYSTERY IN THE SNOW
THE PIZZA MYSTERY
THE MYSTERY HORSE
THE MYSTERY AT THE DOG SHOW
THE CASTLE MYSTERY
THE MYSTERY OF THE LOST VILLAGE
THE MYSTERY ON THE ICE
THE MYSTERY OF THE PURPLE POOL
THE GHOST SHIP MYSTERY
THE MYSTERY IN WASHINGTON, DC

D0167471

✿ ✿ ✿ **Spring Special** ✿ ✿ ✿

THE MYSTERY IN WASHINGTON, DC

created by

GERTRUDE CHANDLER WARNER

Illustrated by Charles Tang

SCHOLASTIC INC.

New York Toronto London Auckland Sydney

Activities by Nancy E. Krulik

Activity illustrations by Alfred Giuliani

No part of this publication may be reproduced in whole or in part, or stored in a retrieval system, or transmitted in any form or by any means, electronic, mechanical, photocopying, recording, or otherwise, without written permission of the publisher. For information regarding permission, write to Scholastic Inc., 555 Broadway, New York, NY 10012.

ISBN 0-590-47534-7

Copyright © 1994 by Albert Whitman & Company. All rights reserved. Published by Scholastic Inc., by arrangement with Albert Whitman & Company. THE BOXCAR CHILDREN® is a registered trademark of Albert Whitman & Company.

12 11 10 9 8 7 6 5 4 3 4 5 6 7 8 9/9

Printed in the U.S.A. 40

First Scholastic printing, March 1994

Contents

CHAPTER 1

Another Adventure!

"That sounds wonderful," Grandfather said heartily. He paused long enough to smile at the four Alden children who were sprawled on the den floor playing Monopoly. "Oh, I'm sure they'll love it," he added, tucking the receiver under his chin. He reached for the scratch pad that Mrs. McGregor always kept by the telephone in the kitchen. "Let me get a few directions from you . . ."

"Is Grandfather talking about us?" ten-year-old Violet whispered to her older sister, Jessie, who was twelve.

"I think something's up," six-year-old Benny said confidently. "Something big." He landed on Park Place and whooped with joy. "Yippee! I already own Broadway, so now I can buy a house!"

"I think Grandfather's planning a trip for us," Henry said thoughtfully. Henry was fourteen and the oldest of the children.

Violet looked up from her neat piles of play money. "You mean another adventure?" Ever since their grandfather had found them living in a boxcar and rescued them, their lives had been one wonderful adventure after another.

"You bet!" Jessie said enthusiastically. "Let's listen."

"Right at the Jefferson Memorial and left at the Reflecting Pool . . ." Grandfather's voice drifted across the room.

"The Jefferson Memorial?" Benny said, wrinkling his nose. "We learned about that in school. But I can't remember where it is."

"I remember," Violet interrupted. "It's in Washington, DC."

"That's right. Washington, DC," Grandfather said as he hung up the phone. "That's the next place you're going to explore — the nation's capital."

"We're going to Washington!" Benny stood up so quickly, his play money fluttered around his feet. "Wow! When are we leaving?"

"My old friend Steve Bagley in Richmond, Virginia, is expecting me tomorrow evening," Grandfather said, settling into his favorite chair. "I figured while I was there it would be a nice chance for you to visit Washington. I've arranged for you to stay with my friend Mrs. Parsons at her B and B."

"What's a B and B?" Benny piped up.

"It stands for Bed and Breakfast," Grandfather explained. "It's not as formal as a hotel and this one's right in the middle of the city."

"I still think it's a funny name," Benny persisted.

"It makes a lot of sense," Henry said. "Because it tells you exactly what you get. It's not a hotel, it's a real house. You get your own room with a bed, and a nice hot breakfast every day."

"That's the best part," Benny said happily. He scrambled into Grandfather's lap.

Grandfather pushed Benny's hair out of his eyes affectionately. "Think you children can get packed in time?"

"I know we can," Jessie said. She immediately began folding the Monopoly board and putting away the pieces. Jessie was the most organized of the Aldens and always liked to keep things neat and orderly.

"How about an early dinner?" Mrs. McGregor, the family housekeeper, poked her head in from the kitchen. "I've heard you have a big trip planned."

"We sure do," Benny said happily. "We're going to Washington . . . uh, DC." He paused. "What does DC stand for?"

"District of Columbia," Jessie told him. She scooped up the empty popcorn bowl and headed for the kitchen.

"Let's go set the table for dinner," Henry reminded Benny gently.

"Okay, but I'm too excited to eat," Benny retorted.

Jessie and Violet exchanged a look and burst out laughing. "I doubt that," Jessie said, ruffling his hair. Eating was one of Benny's favorite activities. "Mrs. McGregor is fixing one of your favorite meals — spaghetti and meatballs."

"Yum!" Benny said appreciatively. "Maybe I can manage a few bites, after all."

Henry chuckled. "I'll be surprised if you don't have seconds."

"Or thirds," Violet added teasingly.

It was early the next morning, when Grandfather and the children loaded their suitcases into the car. They were backing down the driveway, waving good-bye to Mrs. McGregor, when Watch, the family dog, came tearing around the front steps.

"Oh, look, there's Watch," Violet said sadly. "I think he wants to come with us." She loved all animals, but especially Watch.

"He'll be fine with Mrs. McGregor," Grandfather said. He reached over and squeezed Violet's hand. "Mrs. Parsons doesn't allow pets in the B and B."

In the late afternoon, Violet spotted the signs for Washington. "I think we're getting close," she said, checking the map.

"We're going to head down North Capitol Street," Grandfather told her. "Let's see if you can pick out some of the landmarks I told you about."

"I see one!" Jessie shouted. She stared out the window and then flipped frantically through the guidebook. "It's a beautiful building, with a big white dome, and we're coming right up to it. It's . . . oh, my gosh, it's the Capitol!"

"It's just like I imagined it would be," Violet said, with her nose pressed against the glass. "Can we go inside, Grandfather?"

"It's too late today," Grandfather said with a smile. "But you can go on a tour tomorrow morning, if you'd like. There's a lot to see, and right now, Congress is in session."

"Wow," Benny said softly. For a moment,

everyone was silent as Grandfather slowed down for a better look at the Capitol.

"It's so pretty," Jessie said. "I think this is going to be my favorite building in Washington."

"It's certainly one of the most important," Grandfather said. "But wait till you see the White House, the Lincoln Memorial, and the Washington Monument. Does anybody recognize anything else? We're going to turn right at the Reflecting Pool."

"I see the Mall!" Violet said excitedly.

Benny looked puzzled. "What do you mean?" They were driving down a long boulevard flanked by museums.

"The Mall is where all the Smithsonian Museums are," Henry said. "See? There's Air and Space, and the Museum of Natural History . . ."

"I think we should stop right here," Benny suggested. He could see airplanes hanging from the ceiling inside one of the museums and he wanted to take a closer look.

"I'm afraid all the museums are closing

soon," Grandfather said. "Let's get you settled, and then you can start out fresh tomorrow morning."

They turned onto a narrow side street and pulled up in front of a cheerful-looking brick row house. A slender, red-haired woman hurried to the front door to welcome them into a small hallway filled with antiques.

"Come in, James," she said cheerfully. "You must be the grandchildren I've heard so much about. I'm Molly Parsons."

"It's good to see you, Molly," Grandfather said. He introduced everyone and helped the children bring their suitcases inside. After he and Mrs. Parsons had chatted briefly, Grandfather checked his watch. "I've got to get to Richmond before it's too late. Mrs. Parsons will give you dinner each night as well as breakfast in the morning."

"You mean B, B, and D?" Benny asked. "Bed, breakfast, and dinner?"

"That's right," Mrs. Parsons said. "A lot of my guests take all their meals here. And I have a fourteen-year-old girl staying with me. She'll enjoy the company."

"We'll be fine," Henry said as Grandfather hugged everyone.

"Have a good time!" Benny called out.

As soon as Grandfather left, Mrs. Parsons said, "I have your rooms all ready for you — boys in one room, girls in the other."

"And our dinner?" Benny said hopefully. "Do you have that ready, too?"

"Benny loves to eat," Violet explained.

Mrs. Parsons laughed. "Well, you're in luck. Dinner is ready right now." She looked at Benny very seriously. "Of course, you'll have to eat fried chicken, mashed potatoes with gravy, and corn on the cob. Then plenty of homemade apple pie. Do you think you can manage all that?"

Benny looked amazed. "How did you know those were my favorite foods?"

Mrs. Parsons put her arm around his shoulders and steered him toward the dining room. "I raised four boys of my own, and it was just a lucky guess."

A few moments later, they were seated at a long oak dining table with a shy young girl named Amira. She had deep brown eyes and black hair. Jessie noticed that she kept her hands in her lap and stared at her plate.

"Aren't you hungry?" Jessie said, trying to make conversation with her.

Amira shrugged. "I guess I'm a little tired. My father and I just got here today."

"Is your father upstairs?" Violet asked. She was shy sometimes, too, and wanted to put Amira at ease.

Amira looked even more unhappy at the question. "No, I wish he were. He's staying at a hotel because he has a lot of business appointments." She sighed and fiddled with her fork. "He thought it would be fun for me to stay at the B and B while he's at work."

"Why don't you come explore the city with us?" Jessie suggested, touching Amira's arm. "We're going to start bright and early tomorrow morning."

"Are you sure?" Amira brightened. "Wouldn't I be in your way?"

"Of course you wouldn't be," Henry said firmly. "We'll all go sightseeing together. As soon as we unpack tonight, we'll show you our guidebooks. We can plan our first day together."

Amira gave a broad smile. "That would be fun. That would be wonderful," she said, clapping her hands together. "I can't believe I have four new friends."

"We'll have fun together, Amira," Violet said softly. "You'll see."

CHAPTER 2

Welcome to Washington!

"Did you remember to bring the camera?" Violet asked Jessie the next morning. They had just finished a huge breakfast of bacon, eggs, and waffles, and were waiting in the front hallway for the rest of the group to join them.

Jessie patted her shoulder bag. "It's right here, but we need to pick up some film. And I think we'd better buy some stamps. Benny wants to send postcards to Mrs. McGregor, Aunt Jane and Uncle Andy, cousins Joe, Alice, and Soo Lee — everyone he knows."

"If you need stamps, I've got a brand-new roll," Mrs. Parsons said. She was sitting on a high stool behind the reception desk, working on her accounts. She opened her desk drawer and frowned. "Well, that's funny. I could have sworn it was here yesterday."

"We can buy some for you," Jessie offered.

"That would be a big help. I'll give you some money from petty cash." She pulled open another drawer and shook her head in dismay. "Now that's really strange. I know I put a ten-dollar bill in here yesterday. I'm beginning to think that I'm imagining things."

"What are you imagining, Mrs. Parsons?" a young man said good-naturedly. He was tall and thin, with sandy brown hair and glasses.

"Oh, I'm just missing a few things from the front desk. You haven't seen a roll of stamps and a ten-dollar bill, have you, Peter?"

"No, I haven't," he said. "But I was really busy yesterday. There were people coming and going all day long."

"Well, it's not important," Mrs. Parsons reassured him. "I want you to meet our new guests — the Aldens. Jessie and Violet, this is Peter Marshall, my assistant. He does everything for me."

"Mostly, I answer the phone and help out in the kitchen." Peter shook hands with them.

"Peter's a full-time student," Mrs. Parsons said proudly. "He's studying to be an engineer."

"Wow — like on a train?" Benny yelled from the stairwell. He thundered down the last few steps and smiled up at Peter.

"I'm afraid I won't be that kind of an engineer," Peter said as everyone laughed. He bent down so he was on eye level with Benny. "But I'm learning how to design airplanes. So if you want an extra-special tour of the Air and Space Museum, I'll be your guide."

"We're going there tomorrow," Henry said, appearing with Amira.

"Tell you what," Peter said, consulting an appointment book. "I'm free from twelve to two. Why don't we meet in the museum cafeteria at noon?"

Benny's eyes lit up. "The cafeteria sounds great."

Jessie grinned at Peter. "You couldn't have picked a better spot."

"Where shall we start?" Violet said twenty minutes later. "There are so many things to see." They had walked down a leafy side street to the Smithsonian, and had just arrived at the Reflecting Pool. There were four bronze lions surrounding them, and bright sunlight was bouncing off the water. A few people had stopped to feed the seagulls that swooped down, squawking for food.

"It looks like we're at the south end of the Mall," Henry said. "There's the Capitol right behind us, and you see that tall tower in the distance, Benny? That's the Washington Monument."

"Can we go up inside it?" Benny asked excitedly.

"Maybe this afternoon," Jessie said. "But

right now, why don't we take a tour of the Capitol?"

"I want to go way up inside the dome." Benny pointed to the top of the gleaming white building.

"Let's go inside the Rotunda right now," Amira said suddenly. "I think they're starting a tour." She followed a group of tourists through a set of bronze doors and led the way into the Rotunda, a huge circular hall. "I'm afraid you can't go up into the dome, Benny, but look up at the very top. There's a fresco."

Benny arched his head back so far, he nearly toppled over.

"What's a fresco?" He peered upward in amazement. The dome was much bigger than he had realized.

"It's a painting they do on wet plaster," Henry said. "We learned about it in school."

"That's George Washington up at the very top," Amira said, keeping her voice low. The tour guide was explaining that the dome was as high as an eighteen-story building.

"It's beautiful," Violet said in awe. There were intricate carvings and paintings all the way up to the top of the dome. How did someone paint all that? she wondered.

"The artist had to rig up scaffolding and lie on his back," Amira said, as if reading her thoughts. "His name was Constantino Brumidi."

"You really know a lot," Jessie said admiringly.

Amira gave a shy smile. "I'm interested in history, that's all."

After they looked at the Rotunda, Henry and Benny headed for the floors of the House and Senate, while the girls took a look at the Old Senate Chamber.

"It's so little," Violet said in a hushed voice. "It's hard to believe that all the senators could fit in one little room. I guess Congress was much smaller in the old days."

"A lot of important things happened here," Jessie reminded her. "The chamber was a beautiful room, with red velvet carpeting and soft gaslights."

After a while the boys joined them. "We

saw the House floor and the Senate floor, but nobody was there," Benny said. "I thought there would be lots of speeches going on."

"Congress isn't in session today," Amira spoke up. "That's why the flags weren't up outside." When everyone turned to look at her, she explained, "When either the House or the Senate meets, it flies its own flag outside."

"You know the part I liked the best about the Senate?" Benny said as they headed back to the Rotunda. "They had wooden desks, just like you see in school. And I noticed something else," he added, "some of the senators had even carved their initials in them!"

Violet and Jessie laughed. Sometimes Benny had a way of noticing things that no one else did.

Later, on the way to lunch, Violet asked a question and Amira surprised them again by her knowledge. "What's *e pluribus unum* mean?" she asked.

"*E pluribus unum*," Amira said quickly. "That's Latin, Violet. It means 'one out of many'."

"They sure use it on a lot of plaques and decorations."

Amira nodded. "It's what America stands for."

"One out of many?"

"One country out of many states."

"Oh, I get it," Benny said. "That's a good slogan."

"We'll have to take Soo Lee here one day so she can learn about the United States government," said Henry. Soo Lee was a little girl from Korea that cousin Joe and Alice had adopted.

When they were standing in line at the Capitol cafeteria, Violet noticed that Amira seemed a little uneasy. "What's the matter?" Violet joked. "Don't you see anything you like on the menu?"

"Oh, it's not that. It's all looks delicious." Amira pushed her tray next to Violet's, and chose exactly the same lunch — macaroni and cheese.

"Could you hand me those fish sticks, Amira?" Benny asked. He was standing on tiptoe but the plate was just out of reach.

"Sure, but I . . . what did you ask for?"

"Fish sticks," he repeated. "Right there." He tapped the glass window in front of her.

Amira hesitated. "Now I see them. Fish sticks." She reached for a plate of french fries and plunked it on his tray.

Benny looked up at her, puzzled. "I love french fries, but you forgot the fish sticks."

"I'll get them," Jessie said quickly. "Here you go, Benny."

They moved quickly to the cashier, and Amira looked embarrassed. Jessie looked at her new friend thoughtfully. It seemed that Amira had never seen or heard of fish sticks before.

"What does your father do, Amira?" Henry asked when they were settled at a table.

"He's . . . in business." Amira ducked her head and began eating quickly.

"Really?" Henry persisted. "What kind?"

"It's hard to explain," she said slowly. She sounded uncomfortable, and looked nervously at the group. "He's in . . . foreign business. International business."

"He must travel a lot," Jessie said. "It must be fun going with him."

"Oh, I usually don't travel at all," Amira told her.

"What kind of music do you like?" Jessie asked.

"I . . . I don't listen to music," Amira said quickly.

"You don't listen to music?" Benny was amazed.

"No, I don't." Before anyone could ask her any more questions, Amira grabbed the guidebook, and began reading aloud about the Capitol. Violet only half-listened, her mind racing. Amira seemed to know a lot about history, and almost nothing about everyday things. And she obviously didn't want to talk about herself. Their new friend was very mysterious.

Henry was thinking, too. He noticed a pair of men in dark suits who were sitting a few tables away. They were both reading newspapers, but they glanced over at the Aldens every now and then.

Henry knew he had seen them before.

They had been right behind Benny in the cafeteria line. There was nothing unusual about that, he told himself. He relaxed and began eating, and then suddenly it dawned on him. The men in dark suits had been right behind them, strolling up the Capitol steps! And he was sure he had spotted them walking along the same leafy side street toward the Smithsonian. He closed his eyes and tried to remember. Yes, it was definitely them! One had a mustache and one had a funny way of walking with his elbow jutting out. These were the same men.

But why were they following the Aldens? Henry looked over at one of the men just before he ducked his head back behind his newspaper. Yes, there was something going on. They were in the middle of a new mystery!

CHAPTER 3

We're Being Followed!

"Some new guests arrived today," Mrs. Parsons said later that afternoon. "That's why I'm cooking an extra large pot roast." A delicious aroma drifted in from the kitchen.

"May we help you?" Violet offered.

"You can give me a hand with the vegetables and dessert, if you like." Mrs. Parsons led the way to the kitchen. Within minutes, Henry and Benny were busily chopping vegetables, while the girls sliced apples for a crumb-topped pie. "Your father called today," Mrs. Parsons said to Amira.

Amira immediately put down her knife and looked worried. "Is anything wrong?"

"Why, no, of course not." Mrs. Parsons seemed surprised. "He just wanted to make sure you're having a good time."

"Well, I am," Amira said slowly, "thanks to my new friends." Everyone began talking about their visit to the Capitol, and Jessie noticed that Amira seemed happy as long as the conversation didn't revolve around her. She never wanted to talk about herself or her parents. Jessie suddenly realized that she didn't even know whether Amira had any brothers and sisters, and decided to ask her.

Amira immediately looked guarded. "I have two brothers and a sister, but they're back with . . . I mean, they're at home with my mom."

"That's nice," Violet said warmly. She seemed to sense that Amira was uncomfortable.

"What time is dinner?" a voice boomed into the kitchen. Everyone turned to see a large woman in a dark purple dress.

"It'll be ready at six, Mrs. Wentworth." Mrs. Parsons turned and slid a pan of biscuits into the oven.

Mrs. Wentworth consulted her watch. "Well, I hope it's going to be served *promptly* at six," she retorted. "I haven't had a bite to eat since lunchtime."

"I'll be glad to make you a cup of tea," Mrs. Parsons said a little wearily.

"Just concentrate on dinner," Mrs. Wentworth snapped. "That will be quite enough."

"Wouldn't you like to meet the children — " Mrs. Parsons began and then stopped abruptly. Mrs. Wentworth had already swept out of the kitchen.

"Wow," Benny said softly. "Is she going to be eating with us every night?"

Mrs. Parsons bit her lip as though she were trying not to laugh. "Yes, she is, Benny. I'm sure she's very nice . . . once you get to know her."

Mrs. Wentworth barely nodded when she was introduced to the Aldens and Amira, and frowned all through dinner. Luckily there were other guests to talk to, and Violet started a conversation with Mr. and Mrs. Cooley, who were professional photographers.

"I have a new camera," Violet confided, "and I'm still learning how to use it." She was very proud of the camera that Grandfather had bought for her.

"Do you develop your photographs yourself?" Henry asked.

"Yes," said Mrs. Cooley.

"No," said Mr. Cooley at the same time. They looked at each other and laughed nervously.

"What we mean is . . ." Mrs. Cooley began, and her voice trailed off.

"Sometimes we do and sometimes we don't," Mr. Cooley explained.

There was a long silence. Henry was puzzled, but didn't say anything. The Cooleys seemed so uncomfortable talking about their work.

Jessie spent most of the dinner hour talking to John Sudderth, a quiet man from New England who said he was an artist. He seemed to know a lot about Washington, and was enthusiastic when she told him they were visiting the Smithsonian the very next day. "Make sure you visit the Air and Space Museum," he advised her. "It'll be quite an experience."

"We have our own personal tour guide," Benny spoke up. He smiled at Peter Marshall, who brought coffee and apple pie in from the kitchen.

Peter made a thumbs-up sign to Benny. "Air and Space at noon," he said.

"We'll be there!" Benny said happily.

After turning out the lights later that night, Henry glanced out the window. He was sharing a bedroom with Benny at the front of the house, and he had a good view of the tree-lined street. Suddenly he noticed a pair of headlights creeping down the road. Curious, he watched as a long black limousine paused in front of the Parsons's front door, and then slowly moved on. What was the limousine doing? he wondered. And who was inside?

Benny stirred sleepily and sat up in bed.

"Is that the long black car again?" he asked drowsily.

Henry nodded, still staring out the window. "It's a limousine. Have you seen it before?"

Benny yawned. "It passed by the house three times tonight."

Henry turned in surprise. "Are you sure?"

Benny nodded. "I'm positive. I bet it belongs to someone really famous," he said. "Maybe it's the president of another country, and they're looking for the White House."

"Maybe," Henry said thoughtfully. He glanced over at his brother, who had already pulled the covers over his head. Something strange was going on. He was sure of it. First there were the men in sunglasses who seemed to be following them at the Capitol, and now the limousine.

And he also had the feeling that something was wrong at the Parsons'. Mrs. Parsons had reached into her purse for a ten-dollar bill after dinner, and had come up empty-handed. When Jessie had asked her if everything was all right, she had made light of it.

"Things have a way of disappearing around here," she had said.

But was that all there was to it? Henry wondered. She had complained about missing a roll of stamps and some money from petty cash just the day before. And now money was missing from her purse. Was there a thief in the house? Henry turned away from the window and climbed into bed. He decided to talk to Jessie and Violet the next day. If something was going on, everyone needed to be on their guard.

Benny was beside himself with excitement when they arrived at the Air and Space Musuem the following morning. There was a huge DC-3 hanging from the ceiling, and they walked under a model of the Wright Brothers' plane.

"We learned about the Wright Brothers in school," he said, tugging at Jessie's hand. "They flew the very first plane at Kitty Hawk, North Carolina."

"Orville and Wilbur," Amira added quietly. As usual, she seemed to be up on everything.

"Look," Jessie said, reading a plaque. "They only flew for a total of twelve seconds. They went up a hundred and twenty feet into the air and then came down."

"It's amazing they got up at all," Violet pointed out. "See how fragile the plane looks."

"May we touch the moon rock?" Benny asked, darting a few feet away. "The sign says it's okay."

"I guess so." Jessie followed him to a small exhibit near the front door and watched as he touched a flat triangular stone.

"It doesn't feel like anything special," Benny said, looking at his fingertips. "If I saw it lying on the sidewalk, I probably wouldn't even recognize it."

"It's four billion years old," said a guard nearby.

"Wow!" Benny touched it again. "Who found it?"

"It was the Apollo crew," the guard explained.

"I wish I could take a piece of it home with me," Benny said.

The guard laughed. "So do a lot of other people. But I have a better idea. How would you like to take home real astronaut ice cream?"

Benny clapped his hands together. "May I?"

"You can buy it in the gift shop. It's freeze-dried, of course."

"After lunch, Benny," Violet said, pulling him away. "Peter's waiting for us."

The glassed-in cafeteria had a wonderful view of the Mall, and the Aldens and Amira joined Peter Marshall at a long table by the window. Everyone munched on submarine sandwiches while Peter described the Sea-Air Operations exhibit. "It's just like being on a real flight deck, Benny."

"May we go there right now?" Benny was excited.

"I want to take a picture first," Violet said, standing up. "Scoot in close together, everyone." She backed a few feet away from the table. "Smile!" she said as the camera clicked.

"I think I got the Capitol in the background. Oh, darn," she added, "that's the last one on the roll."

"Don't worry," Peter told her. "There's a place around the corner that develops pictures in an hour. We can drop off your film after lunch, and it will be ready this afternoon."

CHAPTER 4

Danger in Air and Space!

After lunch, Peter took everyone to the Sea-Air Operations section of the museum.

"This is fun!" Benny shouted, bounding up the stairs. For the next half hour, he pretended he was commanding the air-traffic control tower of a real aircraft carrier. Everything was painted battleship-gray, and he played with dozens of dials and gauges.

"This seems so real," Amira said, her eyes wide.

Later, when Peter and Amira were looking

at an Amelia Earhart exhibit, Henry drew Violet, Jessie, and Benny aside. "I think we need to talk tonight, when we get back to Mrs. Parsons'."

"I think I know what you're going to say. There's something funny about Amira, isn't there?"

Henry shrugged. "A lot of things about her just don't add up."

"She sure knows a lot," Benny said.

"But there are some things she doesn't know anything about," Jessie said. She had noticed at lunch that Amira was amazed that they could order toppings on their pizza.

"Maybe she's just shy," Violet said. She liked Amira and was happy that they were friends.

"I think it's more than that — " Henry broke off suddenly when he noticed the same two men in dark sunglasses standing behind Peter and Amira. They were back!

"Can we go to the movie?" Benny pleaded, interrupting Henry's thoughts. "There's one starting right now." He pointed to the sign for the "To Fly" show at the theater inside the museum.

"That's a great idea," Henry said, opening his wallet. "Why don't you get in line and get tickets for all of us? Just wave to me when you have them."

As soon as Benny scampered off, Henry turned to Jessie and Violet. "See those two men over there?" he asked in a low voice. "They've been following us."

Violet stared and then gulped. "You're right," she whispered. "I saw them yesterday."

"Are you sure?" Jessie looked uncertain.

"I'm positive. I thought it was really strange that they were wearing sunglasses inside," Henry said. "And Benny saw them, too." Then he told them about the black limousine.

"What can we do?" Violet asked nervously.

Henry looked over at Benny, who was holding a handful of tickets in the air. A "sold out" sign flashed over the ticket window, and Henry grinned. "I think we can lose them," he said. "At least for forty-five minutes."

Moments later, the Aldens were settled in the darkened theater with Peter and Amira.

"This was a great idea," Jessie whispered to Violet.

"I know." Now that they were finally settled, Violet relaxed a little. The men in sunglasses had tried to follow them into the theater, but were turned back because they didn't have tickets. Still, would they be waiting for them outside? The movie started then, and Violet was on the edge of her seat, caught up in the excitement of the show.

When the film ended, Benny felt a little dizzy. Now he knew how a bird felt, swooping off cliffs and plunging into deep canyons.

Jessie blinked a little as they stepped back into the museum. The men in dark glasses were nowhere in sight. Peter had to go to class, and they spent the rest of the afternoon looking at hang gliders and the Charles Lindbergh exhibit.

"Don't forget to pick up your film, Violet," Jessie reminded her. Peter had offered to drop off her film to be developed on his way to class.

"Let's do it on the way back to Mrs. Parsons'. I can't wait to see how they come out!"

The lobby was quiet when they trooped into the Parsons later that day, but a radio was playing softly in the kitchen. "Is that you, Amira?" Mrs. Parsons called. "I have a message for you."

"Please excuse me," Amira said to the Aldens, heading toward the kitchen.

"Let's go upstairs," Henry suggested. "This would be a good chance to talk."

The four Aldens went into Henry and Benny's room and Henry shut the door. "Let's have a look at those pictures," he said.

Violet opened the envelope and flipped quickly through the pictures. Then she stopped. "Just as we thought." Everyone turned to look, and she held up the picture she'd taken in the museum cafeteria.

"What's wrong with it?" Jessie asked, puzzled. Then she gasped. At the edge of the picture, she recognized two figures at a nearby table. The men in sunglasses!

"We've got to get to the bottom of this," Henry said. "They must have been watching us all day."

"Please don't say anything to Amira yet," Violet pleaded. "You know how timid she is. This would just upset her."

"We have to settle this sometime," Henry said grimly.

A light tap at the door made everyone jump. "Is it okay to come in?" Amira said.

Violet exchanged a look with Henry, and he took a deep breath. Maybe his sister was right. Maybe they shouldn't say anything to Amira right now.

"Sure, Amira," he said, opening the door. He carefully slipped the cafeteria picture in his pocket.

Later that evening, Mrs. Wentworth came into the dining room in a terrible mood. "I have an announcement to make," she said loudly. Everyone stopped talking and looked at her. She put her hand to her throat. "My brooch is missing!" she said dramatically.

"I'm so sorry — " Mrs. Parsons began,

but Mrs. Wentworth cut her off.

"I don't care about how sorry you are," she said angrily. "I want my brooch back. It's been in my family for years, and it means a lot to me. It's not expensive, but it belonged to my grandmother. I'll never find another one like it."

"I'll help you look for it, Mrs. Parsons," Violet said when Mrs. Wentworth left the dining room. She quickly began clearing the dinner dishes away, with Benny's help.

"We'll all pitch in," Jessie offered. As soon as the kitchen was cleaned, the Aldens began a thorough search of the hallway, living room, and dining room. Nothing turned up, even when Amira turned over all the sofa cushions, and Benny crawled under the furniture.

"I just can't understand it," Mrs. Parsons said, settling into a wing chair by the window. "I've never had a bit of trouble with thefts, and now something seems to be missing every day."

"When did it start?" Henry asked.

Mrs. Parsons thought for a moment.

"About a year ago, I guess. But it's always been little things, so I didn't think much about it. A few dollars here and there, a roll of stamps. And now this . . ." She cupped her chin in her hands and her voice trailed off.

"Don't worry, Mrs. Parsons," Jessie said soothingly. "We're going to help you find that brooch." She glanced at Amira and the others. "All five of us."

CHAPTER 5

A Trip to the Money Factory

The next morning, Violet went down to breakfast early and found Peter Marshall alone in the dining room, reading the paper.

"Thanks a lot for taking us to the Air and Space Museum yesterday," she said. "We really enjoyed it."

"I had fun, too," Peter told her. He passed her a platter of hot buttered rolls. "There's blackberry jam," he added. "Mrs. Parsons makes it herself."

"It looks great," Violet said. They ate quietly for a few minutes, and then Violet spoke up. "I really felt sorry for Mrs. Parsons last night. Mrs. Wentworth was furious, and she put all the blame on her."

"What do you mean?" Peter looked puzzled.

She quickly told him aout the missing brooch. "And it never turned up," she finished. "We practically tore the living room apart looking for it."

"I . . . I didn't know about any of this." Peter reached for a glass of orange juice. "It's too bad Mrs. Parsons got blamed."

"The sad part is that the brooch isn't even valuable," Violet added.

"It's not?" he asked. "Usually those old-fashioned cameos are collectors' items. They're worth a gold mine."

"Not this one. Mrs. Wentworth said that it's not expensive, but it's been in her family for years."

The other guests then trooped into the dining room for breakfast, and Peter quickly cleared his place. Violet greeted everyone and then excused herself. She wanted to dash upstairs and reload her camera before the day's outing.

As she hurried down the hall, she noticed that the door to room six was open, and she glanced inside. She was surprised to see Mr. Sudderth, the artist, standing by the window. He was staying in room ten right next to hers. What was he doing in someone else's room? she wondered. She walked away quickly before he could spot her. Another puzzle, she thought to herself.

She grabbed her camera and film from her room, and was starting down the stairs when she saw Mr. and Mrs. Cooley coming out of their room. "Oh, I'm so glad I caught you," she said.

Mrs. Cooley immediately looked on her guard. "What are you talking about?" she snapped.

"Well, I . . . I . . ." Violet faltered, feeling embarrassed. Why was Mrs. Cooley so annoyed? "I just meant, I need some help loading my camera, and I hoped you wouldn't mind — "

Mr. Cooley looked worried and reached

for the camera. "Let me see it." He turned the camera over in his hand and exchanged a look with his wife. "I think the first thing we need to do is — "

"Oh, come on," his wife interrupted. "We're going to be late for breakfast." She took the camera out of his hand and returned it to Violet. "I'm sorry, but you'll have to find someone else to help you. We're on a very tight schedule.

Before Violet could say another word, they hurried down the hall. What was all that about? Violet wondered. They acted like they had something to hide!

The children spent the morning visiting the Bureau of Engraving, which Benny called "the money factory." It was at the far end of the Mall, by the Washington Monument.

"Whose picture is on a five-dollar bill?" Violet said playfully as they lined up for the tour.

Benny thought for a moment. "Washington!" Violet shook her head and he tried again. "No, wait, it's Lincoln!"

"That's right," Henry said. "Here's a tougher one. Who's on a fifty-dollar bill?"

"I know that one," Jessie spoke up. "It's Grant. And the United States Capitol is on the back."

"How did you know that?" Benny was impressed.

"Because there's one on display on the wall." Jessie giggled. "I've got a really tough question for you. Who's on a two-dollar bill, Amira?"

Amira hesitated. "That's a trick question. There are no two-dollar bills."

"No, they do exist. You just don't see them much." Henry pointed to a two-dollar bill that was framed and mounted. "See, here's one. It has Thomas Jefferson on it."

Amira nodded. "You're right. I wasn't thinking," she agreed.

With Benny in the lead, they marched down a narrow observation corridor lined with glass walls. From their vantage point, they watched as dozens of workers printed sheets of bright green money.

"Look at all the dollar bills coming off the

press!" Benny shouted excitedly. His nose was squished against the glass. "How come the money is all stuck together?"

"It's not stuck. Money is printed that way," Violet said. "See, there's thirty-two bills on every sheet."

"It would be hard to carry it around like that in your pocket," Benny joked. "You'd have to fold it over and over."

"Don't worry. They're going to cut and trim the sheets into single bills," Violet added.

"Oh, look over here," Jessie said, moving down the line. "They're cutting each sheet in half and . . . I wonder what he's doing?"

They watched as a young man scanned a sheet of bills for defects.

"I think he's inspecting it," Henry said.

"What for?" Benny wondered. "Could somebody make a mistake and print the wrong number?"

"Not the wrong number," Henry explained, "but there could be other mistakes."

"Like what?" Benny was fascinated.

"Well, the dye might be off a little. And

that would make the color too light or too dark." He pointed to a pile of bills that were lying off to one side. They were very pale green.

"I just thought of something." Benny tugged at Amira's sleeve. "How come people can't just make their own money?"

Amira laughed. "Well, for one thing, it's against the law. That's called counterfeit money."

"Like we use in Monopoly?"

"Something like that. Anyway, even if you could print your own money, you'd never fool anyone, Benny. You'd never get it to look exactly right."

Benny frowned, concentrating. "I guess it would be pretty hard to draw all those presidents," he said finally.

"You'd have to be a real artist," Violet told him. "Look at that pretty hand-engraved plate on display. See how perfect each detail is? That's what they use as a model."

They quickly finished the rest of the tour and found themselves on Fifteenth Street, at the west edge of the Mall.

"That was fun!" Benny said, scampering down the steps. "Can we go there next? He pointed to the Washington Monument that was just a couple of blocks away. "It looks like a big exclamation point."

"There are an awful lot of steps," Henry said. He checked the guidebook he always carried with him. "Eight hundred ninety-eight, to be exact."

Benny grinned. "I'm ready."

Amira nudged him. "He's only kidding you, Benny," she said. "There's an elevator."

"Oh, darn, the stairs would be more fun." Benny ran ahead, waiting at the stoplight for the others to catch up with him.

"How long will it take?" Benny asked a few minutes later. They were cramped together inside the elevator that would whisk them to the top of the Washington Monument.

"Only a minute." Henry glanced at his watch.

"Oh, there goes my stomach!" Violet said as the elevator suddenly sprang to life. It seemed to shoot skyward at a dizzying speed,

and then it stopped and the doors flew open.

"That's it?" Benny was hoping for a longer ride.

"Now's the fun part," Jessie told him. "They have viewing windows on the top floor and we can see all of Washington."

Henry and the girls drifted off to look out an east window to the Capitol, and Benny fumbled in his pocket for his toy binoculars. Violet had told him that he could see all the way to Maryland and Virginia if he pointed them in the right direction. He lifted the binoculars, and caught a glimpse of the gleaming white Jefferson Memorial and the Potomac River. Then, with the binoculars still in place, he raced to another window and saw the Lincoln Memorial. "Wow, this is fun," he said out loud. He peered out still another window and did a double-take when he saw a beautiful white mansion. "Ohmigosh!" He stood on tiptoe to get a closer look. "It's the White House!"

He spun around to tell the others when something large and black blocked his view. He took a step backwards, pressing himself against the wall. His fingers trembled on the binoculars when he realized what he was seeing — a man in a dark suit, with sunglasses!

Quick as a flash, Benny darted around him, and headed for Henry and the girls, who had their backs to him.

"Jessie!" he said, when he reached them. "We have to leave. Right now!"

"What's wrong?" Violet asked. "We just got here." But then something in Benny's expression made her freeze.

"Over there," he hissed. "It was one of the men in dark suits. They're still after us!"

Henry spun around, but a group of tourists blocked his view. "Where, Benny?" he asked urgently.

"By that window," Benny whispered, pointing. "He's standing right in front of it."

The crowd cleared then, and Henry started walking rapidly toward the window. He stopped after a few feet, though, and scanned the room. It was too late. The man in the dark suit was gone.

CHAPTER 6

Where's Benny?

"We can't go on pretending nothing's wrong," Violet said later that evening. They had just finished dinner and all four Aldens were sitting in a tiny garden behind the house. "Amira is bound to notice the men in sunglasses herself."

"I'm surprised she hasn't already," Henry said. "They've been trailing us for two days."

"Trailing us, or trailing Amira?" Jessie turned to face him. They were sitting on wrought-iron chairs around a small umbrella table.

"Good point," Henry answered. "We've always been with her, so there's no way to tell."

"Today was a close call," Violet said. She shivered a little even though it was a warm evening. The scene with Benny at the Washington Monument had really shaken her up. The man in sunglasses had been just inches away from Benny — what if he had reached out and grabbed him! The Aldens had stayed calm, finished the tour of the Monument, and then moved on to another museum on the Mall. Amira had never suspected a thing.

Suddenly Peter Marshall called to them from the kitchen. He was holding the screen door open with his elbow and balancing a huge bowl of popcorn. "We're playing cards in the dining room. Want to join us?"

"Sounds great!" Benny bounded to his feet and dashed across the grass. A few minutes later, everyone was settled around the dining room table playing gin rummy.

Violet stopped in the kitchen to get a glass of lemonade, and Mrs. Parsons drew her aside. "Would you mind bringing out some drinks for the others? I'm just too upset to think straight tonight." Mrs. Parsons looked very worried, and was rubbing her hands anxiously on her apron.

"I'll be glad to, but what's wrong?" asked Violet. Mrs. Parsons sat down slowly at the kitchen table, and Violet pulled up a chair next to her.

"There's been another . . . disappearance," Mrs. Parsons said in a low voice. "And this time it isn't money or stamps, it's travelers checks. The Bartletts — the young couple in room six — just came down to tell me."

"Room six?" Violet nearly gasped. John Sudderth had been snooping there that morning!

Mrs. Parsons nodded. "It's such a shame. They say they left them on the dresser, and now they're gone. What could have happened to them?" She glanced toward the dining room. "Surely no one in this house would have taken them."

Violet hesitated. Should she mention that John Sudderth had been in room six? Was he a thief? Or could he possibly have had a good reason for being there? Before she could decide what to do, Peter Marshall called for something to drink, and Violet quickly began making lemonade.

For the next half hour, everyone played cards, and Violet waited for an opportunity to speak to her sister and brothers about John Sudderth. She was all set to duck into the kitchen with them, when Claire Bartlett burst into the dining room.

"It's okay, Mrs. Parsons," she said all smiles. "Look what I found!" She was waving a wad of travelers checks in a navy blue holder.

"Where were they?" Mrs. Parsons looked relieved.

"Somehow they had slipped down between the drawer and the dresser." She smiled at her husband who came up behind her. "You have no idea how much better I feel!"

"Me too," Mrs. Parsons muttered. Violet sank back a little in her seat. At least one mystery was solved!

Later that evening, Jessie was helping Mrs.

Parsons lock up, when she heard a faint mewing at the front door. "Do you have a cat?" Jessie called to Mrs. Parsons.

"Oh, that's Farrah," Mrs. Parsons answered. "Would you let her in for me? She must have sneaked out when I was bringing in the lawn chairs."

Jessie opened the front door and a graceful Siamese cat darted past her legs into the kitchen. She was about to close the door when she heard a car engine idling somewhere on the darkened street. Suddenly the noise became louder and Violet realized that the driver was cruising past the row of brick houses — in the pitch dark! Why would anyone drive with no lights? She pretended to close the door, but kept it cracked open a couple of inches. She watched as a long black limousine paused in front of the Parsons', and then crept slowly down the street. It was impossible to see who was inside because of the darkness, but Violet had a strong hunch.

It had to be the men in sunglasses.

The next day, the Aldens and Amira were

ready to leave the house, when Mrs. Parsons stopped them. "Could you do me a big favor?" she asked. "I could really use a roll of stamps." She handed Henry thirty dollars. "I was sure I had some of the astronaut stamps left, but I can't find them anywhere."

"We'll be glad to get some," Henry told her. He turned and bumped into John Sudderth, who was standing in the hall. "Sorry, sir," he said politely.

"That's okay." The artist's voice was gruff. A batch of letters tumbled out of his jacket. As Henry bent down to help retrieve them, something colorful caught his eye. The envelopes had astronaut stamps on them — just like the ones Mrs. Parsons liked. Was it just a coincidence? he wondered. Why would Mr. Sudderth steal a roll of stamps?

Half an hour later, the Aldens and Amira were strolling down Embassy Row, admiring the colorful flags. "Oh, look," Amira pointed out, "there's the French flag."

"It's red, white, and blue, just like ours," Benny pointed out.

"And there's Italy, England, and Switzerland," Amira added.

"I recognize the Swiss flag," Jessie said. "It's the one with the white cross on the red background. But what's the green one?" She pointed to an unusual flag with a red stripe and a black stripe and an eagle in the middle.

"Oh, that's Egypt." Amira, as usual, was right. When they reached the building, a small plaque said EGYPTIAN EMBASSY.

"You really know a lot about foreign countries," Violet said admiringly.

Amira looked embarrassed. "I'm interested in geography." She quickly lowered her eyes to her guidebook.

"And I see someone who's interested in us!" Benny blurted out. He pointed to a long black limousine that swung around the corner and crawled along the boulevard, keeping pace with them.

They quickly crossed the street, heading to the Smithsonian, and Henry came to a decision. "Amira," he said gently, "a limousine has been following us for days. You don't know anything about it, do you?"

Amira looked startled by his question. "How . . . how would I know anything about it?" she said softly. Two faint spots of color appeared on her cheeks. "There must be hundreds of long black limousines in the city."

"But we keep seeing the same one," Henry said grimly. "The people inside must be after something."

"Maybe they're after us," Benny whispered. He moved a little closer to Violet.

"Are you sure you don't know anything about it?" Henry asked Amira again.

"Yes," Amira said quickly.

"Where shall we go today?" Violet said to change the subject.

"First let's stop here at the Museum of American History," Jessie suggested.

"Where shall we go first?" Amira asked, once they were inside the museum.

"The First Ladies' dresses," Violet said promptly.

A few minutes later, Violet skipped down a red carpet, exclaiming, "I feel like I'm in the White House!" The entrance to the dress exhibit was designed to look like a White House reception room, with crossed flags, crystal chandeliers, and gilt mirrors. They passed under a huge presidential seal and found themselves in a dimly lit maze of rooms filled with mannequins wearing the First Ladies' dresses.

"Look," Jessie said in an awe-struck tone, "there's Mrs. Lincoln's dress. It's beautiful."

"Why is it so dark in here?" Benny said.

"Light damages the dresses," Jessie explained. "Some of the fabrics are very old."

Benny moved restlessly ahead of the others. He was starting to get hungry.

Violet was reading a plaque about preserving the dresses, when she froze. Standing right behind Benny was one of the men in sunglasses! Apparently, he didn't realize that she could see him reflected in the darkened glass.

"Benny," she started to say, but the words caught in her throat when she realized it was too late. Benny had just scampered past a potted fern, and disappeared down another dark corridor. The man in the sunglasses seemed to be following him, and Violet put her hand to her mouth. Should she go after them? Or should she alert the others? There was no time to think!

Just then, Amira edged up to her to look at a dress.

"Listen," Violet said, grabbing her friend's arm. "Go get the others. The men in sunglasses are back, and they're after Benny!"

"What?" Amira looked shaken.

"Just get them!" Violet hissed. Before Amira could even reply, Violet took off at a dead run. She had to get to Benny in time!

CHAPTER 7

Another Theft!

Violet raced past glass-walled rooms filled with mannequins, her heart beating in her throat. Where was Benny? The dim corridors and narrow passages seemed to have swallowed him up. The shadowy halls and smoky glass made everything look scary and confusing. Nothing was what it seemed to be. Violet rounded a corner, and nearly bumped into her own reflection. "Benny!" she cried out anxiously.

"Where is he?" Henry said, running up to her. Jessie, Violet, and Amira were with him, looking pale and frightened.

"I don't know," Violet said. She shook her head hopelessly.

"Ohmigosh! There's one of them," Jessie hissed. She pointed to a man in sunglasses moving swiftly down the corridor. It was impossible to tell where he was heading.

"Jessie, you and Amira head to the right," Henry said urgently. "Come on, Violet, you and I will go the opposite way."

After a terrifying few minutes, Violet spotted a small familiar figure sitting on the floor. "Benny!" She rushed up to him and hugged him. "Are you okay?"

"Of course I am." He looked surprised. "I just got tired of looking at dresses. And I'm hungry, too." He stood up and dusted himself off. "May we go eat lunch now?"

"Oh, Benny! You're safe!" Jessie said as she raced up to her brother, and gave him a bear hug. Benny was more confused than ever. Why was everyone making such a big deal? Even Amira patted him on the head and whispered that she hoped he wasn't frightened. Why would he be frightened?

"I've got a great, idea, Benny," Henry said, looping his arm over his brother's shoulders. "Why don't we have a picnic lunch on the grass?"

"Whoopee!" Benny hooted.

Twenty minutes later, they had settled on a quiet spot in front of the Museum of Natural History. It was a sunny day and some children were playing on "Uncle Beazley," a life-size fiberglass model of a dinosaur.

"That's a triceratops," Benny said confidently. "I have a picture of him in my dinosaur book." He munched on the hot dog and french fries that they'd bought from a vendor. "Can I go play on him?"

"As soon as you finish lunch — " Jessie began, and broke off, laughing. Benny had polished off his hot dog in two giant bites and was already scampering across the grass!

"Stay where we can see you!" Henry called. He watched as Benny joined some other children in a game of tag, and then turned to the girls. "I think we need to talk."

Amira ducked her head, her long dark hair hiding her expression. Violet had been sur-

prised when she had skipped the hot dogs and ordered an unusual-looking food on pita bread. She said it was called falafel and was popular in Middle Eastern countries.

"Those men in the museum, Amira," Henry continued, "you saw them this time, didn't you?"

Amira looked up, her eyes wide. "Yes, but I think you're making too much out of this."

"But they were after Benny!" Violet objected. "You saw what they were up to!"

"I never saw them chase Benny," Amira said quietly. "I think Benny just wandered away, and the men happened to disappear at the same time." She shrugged. "You put four and four together. That's why you jumped to the wrong conclusion."

For a moment no one said anything, and then Jessie giggled. "Four and four? Don't you mean two and two?"

Amira flushed. "Of course, I mean two and two. When I am nervous, I forget . . . I forget what I was going to say."

She seemed so upset that Violet leaned over and patted her arm. "Don't worry,

Amira. Nobody thinks that you have anything to do with those men."

Amira smiled gratefully. "I really do think that you're all worrying too much. Those men would never hurt Benny or any of you. That's the last thing on their minds."

Everyone went back to eating lunch, but Jessie stared at Amira. How could she know what the men in sunglasses were thinking, or planning? Was Henry right? Did Amira know more than she was telling? And what a funny mistake to make — saying four and four, instead of two and two.

After lunch, everyone headed to the west building of the National Gallery of Art.

"I'd like to see the Impressionist paintings," Amira said. "They're always so pretty and full of sunlight."

Minutes later, the Aldens found themselves in front of a colorful landscape painted by Claude Monet. A guide was explaining the painter's style to a group of tourists, and Violet edged forward. Suddenly she spotted a familiar figure in the middle of the crowd.

"Isn't that John Sudderth from the B and B?" she whispered to Jessie.

Jessie stood on tiptoe and peered over her sister's head. "I think so. I bet he spends a lot of time in art galleries, since he's an artist himself."

The Aldens listened for a few minutes as the guide described how the artist made the vivid colors come alive on the canvas.

"But why do they call it impressionism?" a voice interrupted. Violet recognized the speaker. It was John Sudderth.

"That's a good question," the guide said. He gestured to the painting in front of him. "The style was very unusual for the time because Monet painted his *impression* of the scene instead of trying to make it look realistic."

Henry listened intently, frowning. If John Sudderth was an artist, wouldn't he already know that?

The group moved on, and the Aldens stayed behind to admire some paintings of ballerinas by Degas. Violet looked troubled, her mind going back to John Sudderth. What had he been doing in room six the other day? Should she have spoken up, even though the travelers checks had reappeared?

Much later that evening, the Aldens were relaxing over a game of cards when Mrs. Parsons appeared. "This is terrible," she said, sinking into a dining room chair. She cupped her chin in her hands, and looked as though she were going to cry.

"What's wrong?" Violet said, jumping to her feet. She liked Mrs. Parsons and hated to see her upset.

"I'm missing some money from the wall safe," she said quietly. "This time, it's a large sum of money."

"The wall safe?" Jessie asked. "Where is it?"

"It's in the front hall." She shook her head helplessly. "I don't know how anyone managed to break into it. I even had a security mirror installed, so I could keep an eye on it."

"What's a security mirror?" Benny piped up.

Mrs. Parsons turned to Benny. "It's that round mirror on the wall, Benny. It's angled a certain way, so that I can get a good view of the hall, even when I'm sitting behind the reception desk."

"Did they smash the lock on the safe?" Henry asked.

Mrs. Parsons shook her head. "No, so that means they must have known the combination." She sighed and put her hands in her lap. "I'm the only one who knows the combination."

"Don't worry, Mrs. Parsons," Henry said reassuringly. "We'll get to the bottom of it."

"That's right," Jessie added. "You can count on us."

Later, Jessie wandered down the front hall to take a look at the safe. It was built into the wall, a gray metal box with a combination lock in the middle. As far as she could tell, it didn't have any scratches or dents on it. Someone *must* have known the combination, she decided. But who? There were so many suspects — a whole boarding house full of people. Who would want to steal from Mrs. Parsons? She was still thinking about the theft later that night when she heard a familiar, soft rumble outside the front door. She peeked out through the living room drapes and saw the long black limousine creeping down the street.

CHAPTER 8

Sightseeing with Amira

The next morning, the Aldens and Amira gathered in the living room after breakfast to plan their day.

"The museums don't open until ten," Violet said, flipping through a guidebook. "So we have half an hour to decide what to do."

"I know what I want to do!" Benny said, flopping down on the sofa. "I want to go to the insect zoo!"

"You're kidding! You mean there's really a whole zoo filled with insects?" Amira's eyes were wide with surprise.

"It's part of the Museum of Natural History," Jessie told her. "Don't worry. If you don't like creepy, crawly things, there are plenty of other exhibits there."

"We should go to the museum's Discovery Room, too," Henry suggested. He turned to his younger brother. "You'll like it, Benny. They have shells and costumes, and you can play with them as much as you want. They even have a mastodon tooth you can hold in your hand."

"Wow!" Benny said. He bounded to his feet. "Let's go!"

"It's not open yet," Henry reminded him, ruffling Benny's hair.

"I'm going to call the Smithsonian Information Center and double-check the time," Violet said. "The Discovery Room is only open a couple of hours a day." Violet hurried down the hall to Mrs. Parsons's front desk. She sat down, and was reaching for the phone book, when Peter Marshall appeared.

"What do you think you're doing?" he asked angrily. "Get out of that seat right away!"

"I'm sorry." Violet's face was flaming. She quickly stood up and walked around the counter. "I needed to make a phone call, and I didn't think — "

"I don't care what you thought," Peter interrupted rudely. "This isn't your desk, and you had no business sitting here." He brushed past her, hurled himself into the chair, and adjusted his glasses.

Violet stood rooted to the spot, too shocked to move. "If you want to make a call, use the phone in the kitchen," he added, glaring at her.

What's wrong with him? Violet wondered, as she scurried down the hall. Peter had always been so friendly and helpful. Today he was acting like a monster!

"Have fun today," Mrs. Parsons said when the Aldens left half an hour later. Jessie thought she looked sad. She hoped there wouldn't be any more thefts while they were out.

As soon as they stepped outside, Henry was cornered by Mrs. Wentworth, who was armed with a guidebook and an umbrella. "I want to ask you something, young man," she said, drawing him aside. He waited politely on the front steps, while the others moved on down the street.

"Yes, ma'am?"

"I was wondering how much Mrs. Parsons was charging your grandfather for the four of you. Does she give you a discount because you're renting two rooms, or does she charge the full amount?"

The questions caught him off guard. "I . . . I have no idea," he said, embarrassed. Why did she want to know what Grandfather was paying?

"Oh, come on, now," she said in a wheedling tone. "You can tell me." She eyed him shrewdly.

Henry straightened up and returned her stare. "I honestly don't know, ma'am. Maybe you should ask Mrs. Parsons about her rates."

"Humph!" Mrs. Wentworth said disgustedly. "Fat chance she'd tell me anything." She glanced up at the attractive brick house.

"You know, a person could make a pretty penny from this place, if they were smart about it."

"I guess so, ma'am," Henry said. He eyed the others, who were waiting for him at the stoplight.

"Oh, go on, don't let me keep you," Mrs. Wentworth said, dismissing him.

Half an hour later, the children gathered in front of a stuffed, eight-ton African bull elephant in the Museum of Natural History.

"Wow — this is going to be my most favorite place of all!" Benny squealed. He looked around the lobby, his eyes darting over the colorful flags that listed all the collections. Where would they start? Everything looked like fun!

"Dinosaurs, Minerals and Gems, Fossils, Sea Life . . ." Amira said breathlessly. "We could spend all day in here."

"Let's start with this elephant," Henry suggested. He picked up what looked like a phone receiver and handed it to Benny.

"I don't want to call anybody," Benny objected.

"It's not a phone," Henry said with a laugh. "It's a recording."

Benny put the receiver to his ear and jumped when a deep roar blasted out. "It's the elephant!" he said, gazing up at the gigantic animal. He listened intently while everyone watched. "And now they're telling what he liked to eat. Three hundred pounds of grass and plants every day — and he drank fifty gallons of water!"

"And you know something else?" Amira said, reading a plaque. "It took him eighteen hours to do it!"

A couple of hours later, Jessie and Violet collapsed on a bench in the middle of the insect zoo.

"This is fun, but I'm pooped," Violet said, rubbing her feet.

"I'm ready for a break, too," Jessie agreed. "Benny never seems to run out of energy, does he?" She glanced over at her younger brother, who was happily leading Amira toward a cage holding a live tarantula.

"It's feeding time for the scorpion," Henry

said, sitting down next to them. "Anyone interested?"

Jessie shuddered. "I think we'll pass on that."

"I'm glad I have a few minutes to talk to you alone." Henry lowered his voice and looked serious. "Something happened earlier that I think you should know about." He quickly told them about his conversation with Mrs. Wentworth.

"But what did she mean?" Violet asked.

Henry shook his head. "I don't know. She just said you could make a pretty penny from Mrs. Parsons' place."

"Maybe she means you could make money by stealing," Jessie said softly. "Look at all the things that are missing from there!"

"But Mrs. Wentworth lost something herself — her brooch, remember?"

"That doesn't mean anything," Violet objected. "She could have pretended it was missing, just to take attention away from herself."

Suddenly Benny appeared and plunked down next to them.

"Where's Amira?" Henry asked.

"She's buying postcards," Benny said. "She said she'll be right back."

"I don't think the thief is Mrs. Wentworth," Violet went on. "It could easily be John Sudderth. There's something suspicious about him."

"He didn't know anything about art when he was in the National Gallery," Henry recalled. "And he had a bunch of envelopes with astronaut stamps on them — the kind that Mrs. Parsons said were missing."

"There's something else," Violet said quietly. "I never told you this, but I saw him standing in someone else's room the other day. Room six."

"Was he stealing something?" Benny blurted out.

"I don't think so," Violet admitted. "I think he was just looking around."

"Room six!" Jessie said suddenly. "Those are the people who lost their travelers checks."

"Yes, but they found them, remember?" Henry pointed out.

"What about Peter Marshall?" Violet said. "He acted really strange today. He was furious that I was sitting at Mrs. Parsons' desk."

"I wonder why?" Jessie said thoughtfully.

Violet shook her head. "I have no idea. He seemed upset that Mrs. Wentworth's brooch wasn't valuable. He said he thought those old cameos were worth a lot of money."

"He said cameo?" Henry leaned forward. "Are you sure he used that word?"

Violet frowned, trying to remember. "I think he did. Does it matter?"

"It's very important," Henry said. "A cameo is a special kind of brooch. He wouldn't know it was a cameo unless he was the one who stole it."

"Maybe Mrs. Wentworth called it that, and he overheard her," Jessie said.

"That's a good point," Henry admitted. "And the Cooleys — they seem a little suspicious, don't they?"

"They can't even load a camera!" Jessie said. "How can they be photographers?"

"I wondered about that, too," Violet said.

"They acted like they were too busy to help me that day, but I think it was more than that."

"They didn't even know whether they developed their own film or not," Henry added.

For a moment, no one said anything, and then Jessie said shyly, "I really hate to say this, but what do you think about Amira?"

"I like her!" Benny piped up.

"I know you like her, Benny, we all do." Henry lowered his voice. "But we have to face facts. We don't really know much about her. Maybe she's the one being followed by the men in sunglasses." He paused. "I can't believe that Amira is a thief, but until we know for sure, we have to suspect everyone."

"But — " Benny started to object, but Henry put his finger up to his lips. "Everyone," he repeated. "We have to suspect everyone. Let's all remember that."

CHAPTER 9

Thieves in the Night

"I'm afraid there's been another theft," Mrs. Parsons said the following day at breakfast.

"What's missing?" Henry asked. The Aldens and Amira were alone with Mrs. Parsons in the dining room. All the other guests had left to go sightseeing.

"My good china plate," Mrs. Parsons said sadly. "The blue and white one that hung in the lobby. It was hand-painted and went all the way back to the time of Thomas Jefferson."

"I remember it," Violet said softly. "It was pretty."

"When was it taken?" Jessie asked.

"I'm not exactly sure." Mrs. Parsons sat down next to her and poured a cup of coffee. "It was missing this morning, when I opened the front office. But it could have been stolen last night. The reception area was dark when I locked up, and I might not have noticed that it was gone."

"Was it very valuable?" Amira asked.

Mrs. Parsons nodded. "Unfortunately, it was." She glanced at the antique china cupboard next to the window. "You know, I should probably do something about that pair of candlesticks. They're solid pewter — a thief would love to get his hands on them."

"You should hide them somewhere," Jessie said.

"But where? She can't use the safe," Violet pointed out.

"You're right, Violet," Mrs. Parsons agreed. "But I could put them someplace where no one would ever think of looking."

"Where would that be?" Benny scratched his head.

Mrs. Parsons smiled. "The kitchen pantry."

Later that morning, the Aldens were back at the Museum of Natural History, looking at the Minerals and Gems collection.

"Wow!" Benny said, looking at a cube of pyrite. "It looks just like solid gold."

"It's called fool's gold, Benny," Violet explained. "It looks like the real thing. But I like amethyst the best." Violet was admiring a giant block of lavender crystals. The glass display case was dark, except for the glowing stones, and Violet could see Amira and Benny moving behind her. *It's just like a mirror,* she thought to herself. *I can see everything that's going on behind me. I've been in this situation before,* she realized. *This reminds me of something . . . but what?*

The Aldens spent the rest of the day at the Smithsonian, and ate a late supper that night at the B and B. Violet noticed that the pewter candlesticks were missing from the dining room, and she was glad that Mrs. Parsons had decided to move them to a safe place.

Jessie was quiet at dinner, and stared at the guests gathered around the dining room table. Mr. and Mrs. Cooley, Mrs. Wentworth, John Sudderth, Peter Marshall . . . was it really possible that one of them was a thief? When she passed Amira a slice of apple pie, their eyes met for a moment. Could Amira, their own friend, be a thief? *Never!* she thought loyally.

Violet woke up suddenly that night, her heart pounding. She glanced over at Jessie, who was sitting straight up in bed. The room was dark, and the bedside clock said 2:00 A.M. "Jessie, what's wrong?" she hissed.

Jessie put her finger to her lips and padded quietly over to her sister. "Didn't you hear that noise? Someone's rummaging around downstairs. I think we should tell the boys."

Violet pulled her robe around her and followed her sister down the hall to the boys' room. Henry had already turned on his lamp, and Benny was perched on the edge of his bed. "You heard the noises, too?"

Henry asked when he saw the girls.

Jessie nodded, and put her arm around Benny as the four Aldens made their way softly to the door of the room. They stood there listening to the noise from below. The entire house was dark. "What should we do?" Benny asked.

"Should we wake Mrs. Parsons?" suggested Violet.

As they peered down the hall, something soft and furry wound itself around Violet's leg! "Oh!" she gasped.

She heard Jessie giggle behind her. "It's only Farrah, the cat," she whispered.

Just then a shadowy figure rushed by, and they heard a door shut somewhere down the hall. Who was it?

A moment later, Henry and Benny burst through the sliding door that led to the kitchen. "They got away, didn't they?" Henry said, flipping on the light switch. Violet nodded.

"There was someone down here all right," Jessie said. "But we couldn't get a look at them."

"Do you know whether it was a man or a woman?" they asked.

Violet shook her head. "It was impossible to tell."

Benny moved closer to his sister. "What do we do now?"

"In the morning we'll tell Mrs. Parsons. But let's try to get some sleep now," Jessie said. "Tomorrow's our last full day in Washington."

"You mean today," Violet pointed out. "The sun will be up in a couple of hours."

At breakfast, they told Mrs. Parsons what had happened. "I'm not a bit surprised," she said.

"Was something else stolen?" Henry asked.

"No, but the lock on the pantry was broken. Someone was after the candlesticks. Luckily, I changed my mind and hid them in the laundry room!"

That morning, the Aldens were looking at a collection of antique clocks in the Museum of American History. Benny was fascinated by an old-fashioned wooden school clock.

"Doesn't that look just like the one in Mrs. Parsons' kitchen?" he asked.

Jessie leaned over the railing to read the plaque. "It sure does," she said, peering at the clock. "It's very rare. There were only a hundred or so clocks made like that one."

"And it's very expensive," Amira pointed out. "Do you think the one in Mrs. Parsons kitchen is a copy?"

"I don't know," Henry said. "But I think we should tell her as soon as we get back."

After seeing so many museums, the children decided to spend the afternoon at the National Zoo. There they saw all their favorite animals, and even a pair of extra special ones — pandas!

"They look like they're wearing black masks," said Benny.

"These pandas are from China," said Jessie.

"China's right next to Korea, where Soo Lee is from," Violet pointed out.

"That's right," said Henry.

As they strolled around the zoo, Violet

suddenly realized what had been troubling her in the Minerals and Gems exhibit. She had been staring into the darkened glass and could see what was going on behind her. Now it came to her! It was exactly like the time she had sat down at Mrs. Parsons' desk to make a phone call. She had glanced up into the "security mirror" and could see what was behind her — the wall safe! Whoever sat in that chair had a perfect view of the safe . . . was that why Peter Marshall had been so furious with her? Had he sat in that chair and watched as Mrs. Parsons twisted the combination lock and opened the door? Was he the thief? Was he afraid that she would guess the truth?

Violet waited until they were alone after dinner that night to talk it over with Jessie, Henry, and Benny. Amira was downstairs helping Mrs. Parsons, and the Aldens were gathered in the boys' room.

"Do you really think it could be Peter?" Jessie asked. "He seems so nice."

"I think it's a possibility," Henry said

slowly. "Everyone likes him, but still . . . he has the perfect opportunity."

"And the thefts started a year ago," Violet said. "Right around the time he moved in here."

"I think we should talk to Mrs. Parsons in the morning," Henry said. And then they all went to bed.

It was shortly after midnight when Violet heard the noise. She tried to blot it out by burying her head in the pillow, but it was no use — someone was downstairs!

"Jessie, wake up!" She shook her sister lightly, still listening intently. She was positive she heard people talking.

"What's wrong?" Jessie asked groggily.

"The burglar's back," Violet whispered, heading towards the door.

The girls ran into Henry and Benny's room. "We heard it too," Henry whispered. "This time, let's put the light on in the hall. That way, we'll see them when they try to sneak back upstairs." No lights were on downstairs, which meant whoever it was was poking around in the dark. Violet's heart pounded as they waited, huddled in the doorway. At last they heard footsteps padding up the stairs. The footsteps came down the hallway, closer, closer . . . at last they reached the door. It was the Cooleys!

Henry stepped into the hall.

"Oh, you scared us!" Mrs. Cooley cried. She was dressed in a bathrobe.

"What were you doing down there?" Henry demanded.

"Well, we . . . went down to get a snack," Mrs. Cooley said. She quickly shoved a small camera into the pocket of her robe.

"In the dark?" Henry persisted.

"We couldn't find the light switch," Mr. Cooley spoke up. He was holding a flashlight. "We thought we'd just make a quick sandwich and go back upstairs." He exchanged a look with Mrs. Cooley.

Mrs. Cooley managed a weak smile. "I wasn't really hungry, after all. I'm just going to turn in." She turned to the Aldens and yawned. "Have a good sleep, now." She and

Mr. Cooley hurried to their room, leaving the Aldens more puzzled than ever.

"What were they really up to?" Violet asked.

"I don't know," Henry replied. There was nothing else the children could do but go back to bed.

CHAPTER 10

The Mystery Is Solved

The following morning Amira joined the Aldens in Benny and Henry's room after breakfast.

Jessie filled Amira in on what had happened the night before.

"Do you think the Cooleys are thieves?" asked Amira. "If not, what were they doing in the kitchen last night? We know they weren't there for a snack!"

"And they claimed to be photographers, but they didn't know how to put film in my camera," Violet added.

"You're right," Amira said. "They're not photographers at all. I talked to them last night at dinner. They're antique dealers, and they travel all over the country looking for unusual items. They noticed that school clock in Mrs. Parsons's kitchen and were planning to take a picture of it. They thought one of their customers might like to buy it."

"But why didn't they do it in the day-time?" Benny asked.

"Probably because they didn't want Mrs. Parsons to know it was valuable," Amira explained. "This way, they could buy it from her at a much better price."

"Well, that explains that," said Henry.

"And I figured out the truth about Mrs. Wentworth," Benny said suddenly.

"You did?" Violet and Jessie chorused.

"She's going to open her own B and B. She told me at breakfast!" Benny looked very pleased with himself.

"So that's why she was so nosy," Henry said. "And why she said someone could make a pretty penny out of Mrs. Parsons' place."

"What about John Sudderth?" Jessie said.

"Remember when you saw him standing in room six?"

"I asked him about that this morning," Violet explained. "He was just admiring the view of the Washington skyline. He wants to use it on a series of billboards he's designing."

"Billboards?" Henry asked.

Violet nodded. "He's a commerical artist." She grinned. "That explains why he didn't know that much about fine art that day in the museum."

"That only leaves Peter Marshall," said Henry.

"I wish there was some other explanation," Violet said sadly. She liked Peter, and hated to think that he was involved in the thefts.

Henry took a deep breath. "I think we should talk to Mrs. Parsons right now. Peter's almost finished serving breakfast, and we need to catch him before he dashes off to class."

"I think you're right." Jessie led the way downstairs.

"This is hard to believe," Mrs. Parsons

said a few minutes later in the kitchen. Henry had just told her about Peter and the security mirror, and she glanced at the swinging door to the dining room. "What will I say to him? How can I accuse him?"

Just then, Peter appeared carrying an empty platter. "We're running a little short on waffles," he said cheerfully. "Shall I make some more batter?" He noticed the Aldens standing by the stove. "Why aren't you in the dining room? Aren't you hungry?"

"Sit down, Peter," Mrs. Parsons said. Her voice was surprisingly strong. While the Aldens stood silently by, she told him exactly what they had just told her. When she finished, Peter looked pale and shaken.

"I wish . . . I didn't think — " he began and then stopped.

"Peter, just tell me the truth," Mrs. Parsons urged him. She rested her hand on his arm for a moment. "Are you the one who's been taking things from the house?"

There was a long silence while Peter tried to compose himself. "Yes," he said. "I'm afraid so."

"Oh, Peter," Mrs. Parsons said softly. "Why? Why did you do it?"

"It's hard to explain," he began. He looked miserable. "I never thought you'd notice . . ."

"You didn't think I'd notice money missing from the safe? Or my good Jefferson plate?"

"I thought I could replace the money before you looked in the safe," he said. "And the Jefferson plate isn't gone forever. It's at the pawn shop. I was going to get it back for you, just as soon as I had the money."

"But why did you do it?" Mrs. Parsons looked bewildered. "Why would you steal from me?"

"There's no excuse for what I did," Peter said flatly. "None at all." He paused. "But I honestly never meant to hurt you. I didn't have enough money to pay my tuition this semester, and I didn't know what else to do. I was so desperate, I even took a roll of stamps out of your desk."

"Peter, I would have loaned you the money. Gladly."

Peter gave a sad smile. "I realize that now. I should have come to you right away. I can't believe I did such a stupid thing."

Mrs. Parsons thought for a moment. "You didn't just steal from me, you know. What about Mrs. Wentworth's brooch, and that young couple's travelers checks?"

"The brooch is at the pawn shop." He looked embarrassed. "I took the travelers checks, and then I felt so guilty, I put them back behind the dresser."

"Peter, I just can't believe you did this." Mrs. Parsons looked like she was ready to cry.

"It was a mistake," he said earnestly. "A terrible mistake. You've been so kind to me, and I let you down."

Mrs. Parsons stood up. "Well, we have to figure out how to straighten out this mess. I think the first thing you need to do is apologize to Mrs. Wentworth. I'll loan you the money to get her brooch back from the pawn shop."

"You will?" Peter stood up, too. "Aren't you going to call the police?"

Mrs. Parsons patted him on the shoulder. "I don't know, Peter. You've made a bad mistake. Perhaps you could make it up by working extra hours. In the meantime, this afternoon, let's sit down together and see how much money you need for the rest of your schooling. We can work out a loan from the bank."

"Thank you, thank you," he said, squeezing her hand. "I won't let you down again — I promise."

After a busy day of sightseeing, Amira and the Aldens made their way back to Mrs. Parsons's. "At least the mystery has been solved," said Jessie.

"Yes, but . . ." Amira began. "*I* have a confession to make, too." They turned the corner onto the Parsons' tree-lined street.

"You do?" Violet stared at her. "But Peter Marshall confessed to the thefts!"

Amira laughed. "Oh, I didn't steal anything. But I haven't been completely honest with you."

"I knew there was something funny about

you," Benny said. "You couldn't tell fish sticks from french fries!"

"You're right, Benny," Amira admitted. "That's because I had never seen them before."

"Wow!" Benny said softly. "Where are you from?" He couldn't imagine a place without fish sticks and french fries.

"I'm from Egypt — very far from here, Benny," Amira explained.

"We have a cousin, Soo Lee, who's from faraway, too," said Benny.

"But why didn't you tell us?" Violet asked. She felt hurt that her friend had lied to her.

"I wanted to see what it was like to live a normal life for a couple of weeks. My father works for the embassy, and I've always been very protected. I've never been able to come and go as I want, so I asked my father if I could be on my own for a few days. He agreed, but only if I had security guards."

"The men in sunglasses!" Benny exclaimed.

"Yes, they were hired by my father to look after me. I'm sorry they frightened you." She touched Violet's arm. "I wanted to tell you not to be afraid of them, but then you would have known my secret."

"Did you enjoy your freedom?" Henry asked teasingly.

"I loved every minute of it," Amira said. "Especially going sightseeing with my new friends. I'll always remember you when I think of Washington, DC."

"Look, there's the limousine!" Benny cried. "It's right in front of Mrs. Parson's."

"That's my father," Amira said, walking more quickly. "He's come by to pick me up. I want you to meet him."

A few minutes later, all the Aldens met Amira's father, a friendly man with dark hair and flashing eyes.

"Thank you for taking such good care of my daughter," he said solemnly. "I'm afraid we must leave now. Your suitcases are in the trunk, Amira."

"We're going to miss you," Violet said impulsively. She scribbled her address on a piece of paper, and handed it to Amira, who was getting into the back seat. There were

two men in sunglasses in the front seat.

Amira looked at the note and smiled. "I'll write to you!" she promised.

"There's Grandfather!" Benny shouted just then. He pointed to a familiar car that turned the corner and pulled up to the curb.

"Grandfather! It's so good so see you!" Jessie and Benny hugged their grandfather before he was even out of the car.

"I hope everyone had a good time," Mr. Alden said, climbing out and embracing Violet and Henry.

"We did, we did!" Benny chanted. "And we solved two mysteries."

"Two mysteries?" Grandfather asked. "I'm really impressed."

"We didn't really solve the mystery about Amira," Violet pointed out. "She explained it to us."

"It still counts," Benny insisted. "Doesn't it, Grandfather?"

"Well, I'm not sure," Grandfather said, walking up the steps. He smiled. "But I can't wait to hear about it . . ."

GERTRUDE CHANDLER WARNER discovered when she was teaching that many readers who like an exciting story could find no books that were both easy and fun to read. She decided to try to meet this need, and her first book, *The Boxcar Children*, quickly proved she had succeeded.

Miss Warner drew on her own experiences to write each mystery. As a child she spent hours watching trains go by on the tracks opposite her family home. She often dreamed about what it would be like to set up housekeeping in a caboose or freight car — the situation the Alden children find themselves in.

When Miss Warner received requests for more adventures involving Henry, Jessie, Violet, and Benny Alden, she began additional stories. In each, she chose a special setting and introduced unusual or eccentric characters who liked the unpredictable.

While the mystery element is central to each of Miss Warner's books, she never thought of them as strictly juvenile mysteries. She liked to stress the Aldens' independence and resourcefulness and their solid New England devotion to using up and making do. The Aldens go about most of their adventures with as little adult supervision as possible — something else that delights young readers.

Miss Warner lived in Putnam, Connecticut, until her death in 1979. During her lifetime, she received hundreds of letters from girls and boys telling her how much they liked her books.

Springtime Fun with the Boxcar Children

The Boxcar Children are very good at solving mysteries. Now it's your chance to try to solve this mystery. In what *two* places can you find the President of the United States, the National Air and Space Museum, the Lincoln Memorial, the Washington Monument, and a dinosaur skeleton? You don't have to be a super sleuth to solve this mystery — the answers are Washington, DC, *and* in these activity pages!

It's Puzzle Time!

You *and* your pencils will have to be sharp to solve these puzzles!

The Great Bed and Breakfast Mix-up

The Boxcar Children make sure they eat a good breakfast at the Bed and Breakfast before they start their sightseeing. The meal is delicious, but there sure are some odd things happening. Can you find all the things that are wrong with this picture?

The Washington Wordsearch

Violet has made a list of things she wants to see in our nation's capital. Hidden in this wordsearch are things that can be found around Washington, DC. The words are hidden up, down, backwards, sideways, and diagonally. Look for the words that are in capital letters:
White HOUSE, CHERRY trees, the PRESIDENT, CONGRESS, LINCOLN Memorial, MALL, Reflecting POOL, VIETNAM War Memorial, CAPITOL Building, FLAG, SENATE, Supreme COURT, SMITHSONIAN Institution, LIBRARY of Congress.

```
R T S S H O U S E L A
S N M O P C N S L I B
T E I E K H T E I B P
E D T D Y E A R N R O
T I H I C R N G L A O
A S S E V R O N O R L
N E O R R Y P O L Y I
E R N T R U O C M P N
S P I U L P I A A Z C
F L A G K D N A L V O
N Y N B U T R W L L L
N E V E E A M O I D N
L O T I P A C E L J V
I I V S L L Y A B P R
```

Some A-maze-ing Sights!

Washington is full of so many exciting things to see and do! Henry wanted to see the Washington Monument. Now Jessie really wants to see the Lincoln Memorial. Follow the maze and help her get there.

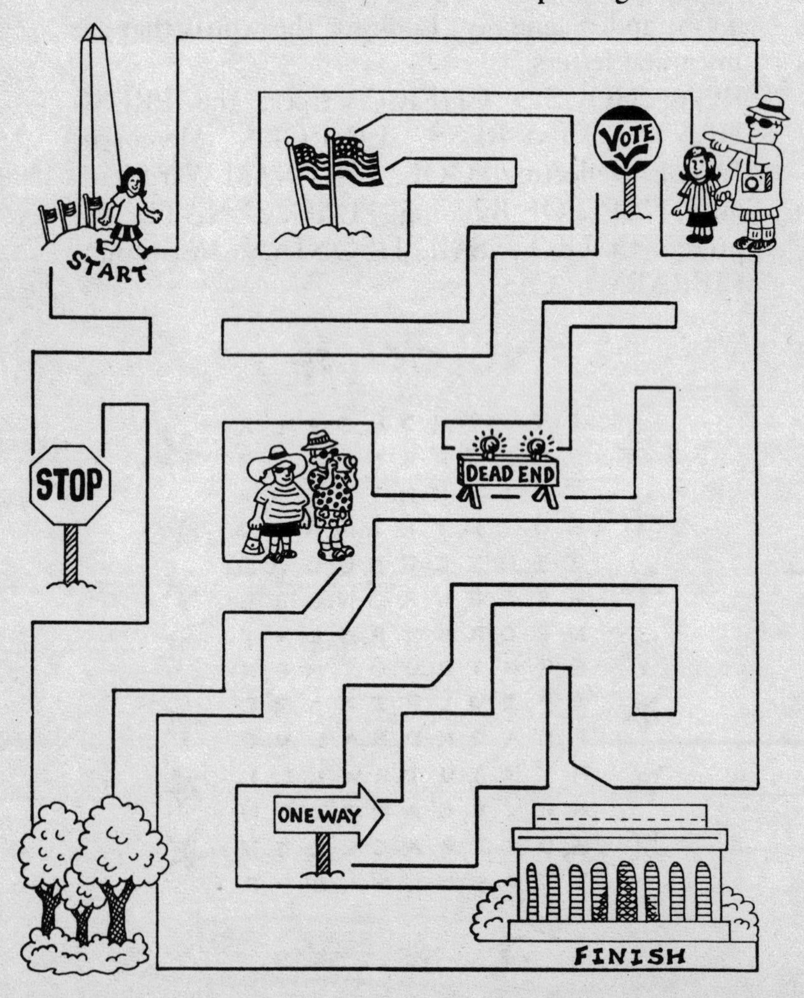

Hail to the Chief!

In 1800, John Adams became the first president to live in the White House. Since then, every United States president has called 1600 Pennsylvania Avenue (the White House's address) home. Can you unscramble the names of nine of our presidents?

ROVOEH ________________
TLICNON ________________
RGNAT ________________
NCOLNLI ________________
ENENDYK ________________
FLRMOEIL ________________
HBUS ________________
AOCJSKN ________________
TELRY ________________

Flying High!

Whenever Benny goes to a national monument, he sees the same thing flying high in the air. To find out what that is, count by fives to connect the dots.

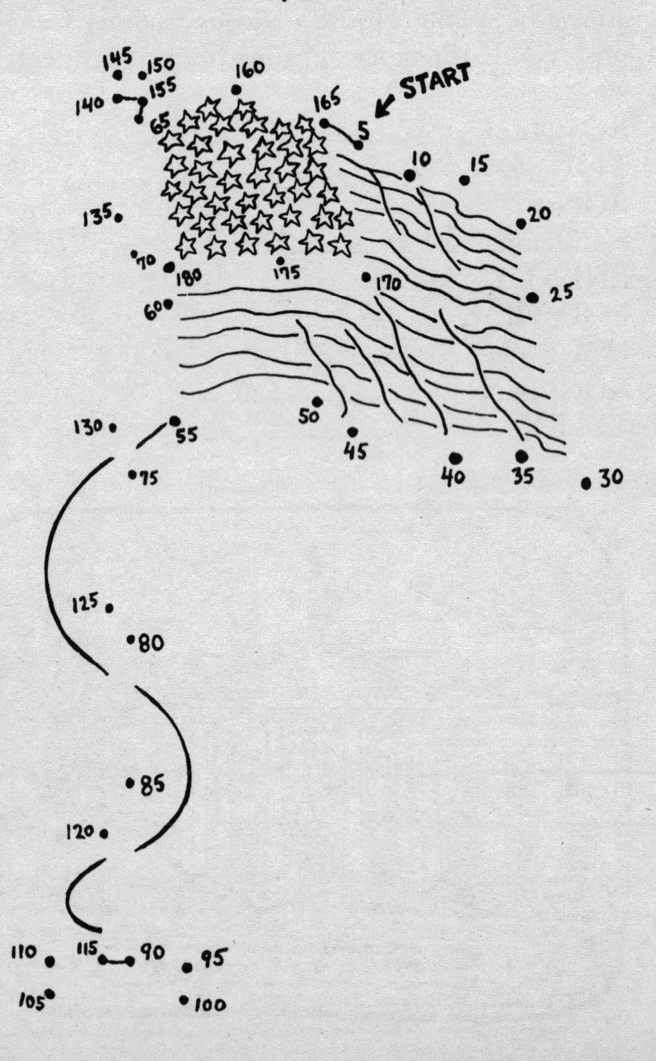

I C U

Jessie and Violet love looking at the First Ladies' Dresses exhibit in the Smithsonian Institution. But Benny has another exhibit in mind — at the Museum of National History. Color in the areas that are marked with vowels, and you will see what Benny is thinking of.

Come and Get It!

At the Bed and Breakfast, Mrs. Parsons cooks for Henry, Jessie, Violet, and Benny. But when the Alden children are on their own, they cook for themselves. Here are two of their favorite pancake recipes. Ask an adult to cook you up a stack of hotcakes, and the rest is up to you! (These yummy recipes work just as well with waffles, too!)

Apple-y Ever After Pancakes

You will need:
a stack of 3 pancakes
1 scoop vanilla ice cream
3 thin apple slices
cinnamon

Here's what you do:
Place one apple slice on top of each pancake. Stack the pancakes so that you have pancake, apple, pancake, apple, pancake, apple. Top with ice cream and sprinkle on a small dash of spicy cinnamon.

Anna Banana Pancakes

You will need:
a stack of 3 pancakes
peanut butter
one banana, thinly sliced
melted butter

Here's what you do:
Spread peanut butter on each pancake. Top each peanut-buttered pancake with a few banana slices. Restack the pancakes, and top with melted butter.

Cool Crafts!

When the Alden children lived in their little red boxcar, they took ordinary objects and turned them into *extra*ordinary things. Now the kids live in a real house with their grandfather, but they still have terrific ideas for great things to make. Here are some of their favorites!

A Balloon Rocket

Henry loved seeing the airplanes and model rockets at the Air and Space Museum. And as soon as he gets home, he's going to make a rocket himself. Here's how.

You will need:
a paper bag
crayons
tape
a drinking straw
string
two chairs
1 long balloon

Here's what you do:
Color the bag to make it look like a rocket.

Flatten the bag. Tape the straw lengthwise on the middle of one side of the bag. Thread the string through the straw.

Tie the string to two chairs. Move the chairs far enough apart so that the string is stretched tight.

Blow up the balloon, but don't tie the end. Use your fingers to keep it closed. Place the round, sealed end of the balloon into the bag.

Let go of the balloon and . . . BLAST OFF!

Looking Like the Pandas!

Violet loved watching the beautiful pandas munch on their bamboo at the National Zoo. As soon as she gets home, she will make this pretty panda mask.

You will need:
a paper plate
a hole punch
black construction paper
scissors
glue
red construction paper
2 6-inch pieces of black or white yarn

Here's what you do:
1. Use the hole punch to make holes in the paper plate where your eyes will be. Place the plate over your face and make sure you will be able to see when you are wearing your mask.
2. Punch a hole where your mouth will be.
3. Cut two panda ears from the black paper.
4. Glue the ears to the top of the paper plate.

5. Cut two doughnut-shaped circles from the black paper. Glue the doughnuts around the eyeholes you cut in the paper plate.
6. Cut a small triangle from the black paper. This will be the panda's nose. Glue the nose to the center of your mask.
7. Cut a smiling mouth with a hole in the center from the red paper. Glue the mouth to your mask over the mouth hole you made in step 2.
8. Use the hole punch to punch one hole on each side of the mask.
9. Loop one piece of your yarn through one of the holes. Make a knot. Loop the other piece of the yarn through the hole on the other side of your mask. Knot that end, too.
10. Put your mask over your face. Have a grown-up tie the two pieces of yarn together so that the mask fits comfortably.

You make a grand panda!

More Great Ideas from the Boxcar Children

The fun isn't over yet! Here are a few more activities the Boxcar Children want to share with you!

What Did You Say?

When great detectives (like the Boxcar Children) are working on a case, they sometimes have to give each other secret information. What better way to keep a secret secret than by using this special language?

Here's what you do:	**Example**
Divide any word into syllables.	Box · car
Say the first syllable without the first consonant.	ox
Attach the consonant to the end of the first syllable, and add the sound *eeda*.	ox · beeda
Now do the same thing with the second syllable.	ar · ceeda

So the word "boxcar" would be *oxbeeda-arceeda*.

If the syllable begins with a vowel, just add *eeda* to the end of the syllable. If the word is a one-letter word, just add *eeda* to the end of the word.

Now, you try and figure out what this secret message says:
Ooheeda-ayreeda! Ouyeeda igfeeda-uredeeda iteeda outeeda!

The Stamp of Approval

A missing roll of stamps is just one clue in this Boxcar Children mystery. But the fun of stamp collecting is no mystery to more than 20 million Americans! And they are not alone — Queen Elizabeth of England has a stamp collection, too. And several American presidents have also collected stamps.

A really quick way for you to start your own stamp collection is to collect all of the cancelled stamps that come into your house. Another way is to go to the post office and buy American stamps. If you want to collect stamps from other countries, you will have to go to a stamp store. You can find rare stamps at stamp conventions. Beware — rare stamps can cost a fortune. In 1981 a five-cent blue Alexandria United States cover stamp sold for more than one million dollars!

No matter what stamps you decide to collect, keep them in good shape. The United States Post Office recommends you store your stamps in an album — under clear plastic or in special stamp hinges. Don't glue or tape them.

One thing's for sure — starting a stamp collection will help stamp out boredom!

Fun Facts About the Presidents

Amaze your friends with the fun things you know about these presidents of the United States!

* Andrew Jackson was the first president born in a log cabin.

*Martin Van Buren was our shortest president. His friends nicknamed him Little Van. Before he became president, Martin Van Buren was a lawyer, and he would sometimes have to stand on tables to talk to the jury.

* President John Tyler had fifteen children. He was playing marbles with some of them when he got the message that he had become president.

* Grover Cleveland was the only president to get married in the White House.

* The teddy bear is named for Theodore "Teddy" Roosevelt.

* Calvin Coolidge had a pet raccoon named Rebecca, which he walked on a leash!

* Harry Truman was the first president to give a speech on television.

* President Gerald Ford was an all-star football player in college.

* President Bill Clinton is also a musician. He plays the saxophone. He likes it when people call him Elvis, after his favorite singer, Elvis Presley.

Answers to the Puzzles

The Great Bed and Breakfast Mix-up

The Washington Wordsearch

R T S S H O U S E L A

S N M O P C N S L I B

T E I E K H T E I B P

E D T D Y E A R N R O

T I H I C R N G L A O

A S S E V R O N O R L

N E O R R Y P O L Y I

E R N T R U O C M P N

S P I U L P I A A Z C

F L A G K D N A L V O

N Y N B U T R W L L L

N E V E E A M O I D N

L O T I P A C E L J V

I I V S L L Y A B P R

Some A-maze-ing Sights!

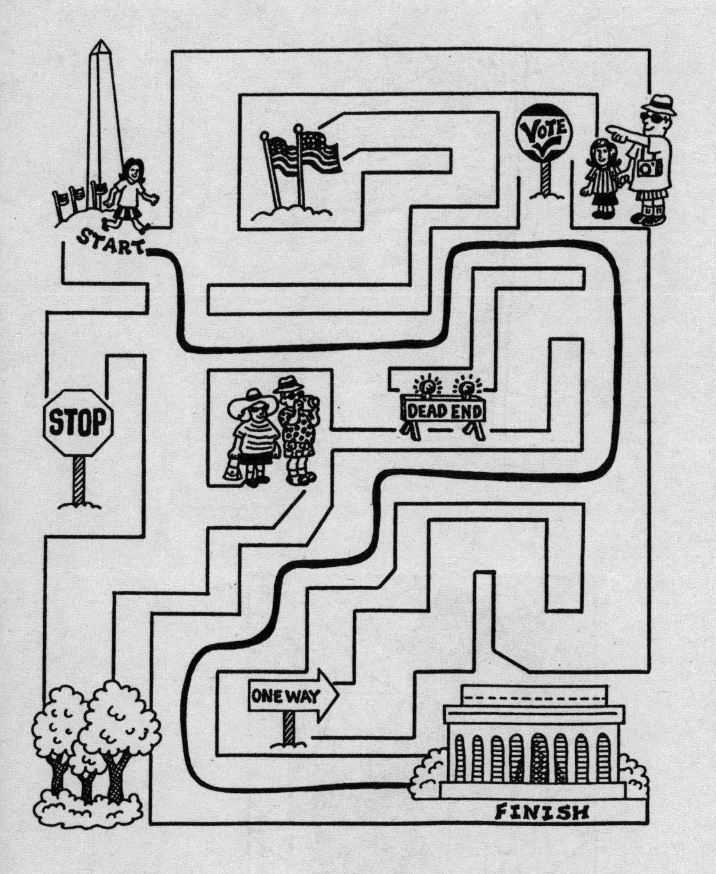

Hail to the Chief!

Hoover, Clinton, Grant, Lincoln, Kennedy, Fillmore, Bush, Jackson, Tyler

Flying High!

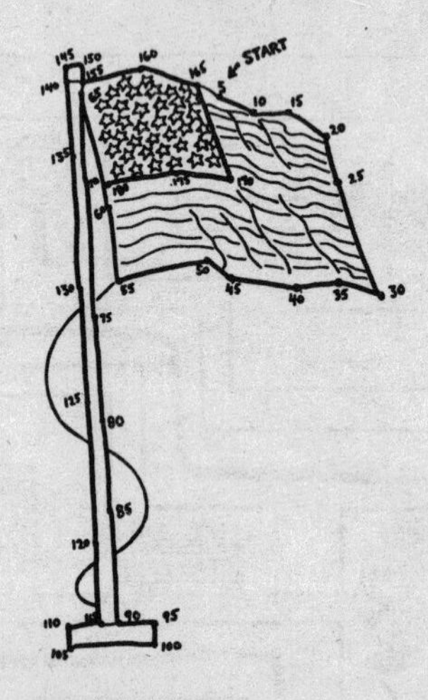

ICU

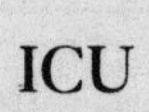